First published in Great Britain 2023 by Farshore
An imprint of HarperCollins*Publishers*
1 London Bridge Street, London SE1 9GF
www.farshore.co.uk

HarperCollins*Publishers*
Macken House, 39/40 Mayor Street Upper,
Dublin 1, D01 C9W8, Ireland

Written by Emily Stead

ISBN 978 0 00 853719 7

Printed in Romania
001

A CIP catalogue record for this title is available from the British Library.

Parental guidance is advised for all craft and colouring activities. Always ask an adult to help when using
glue, paint and scissors. Wear protective clothing and cover surfaces to avoid staining.

Stay safe online. Farshore is not responsible for content hosted by third parties.

Farshore takes its responsibility to the planet and its inhabitants very seriously.
We aim to use papers from well-managed forests run by responsible suppliers.

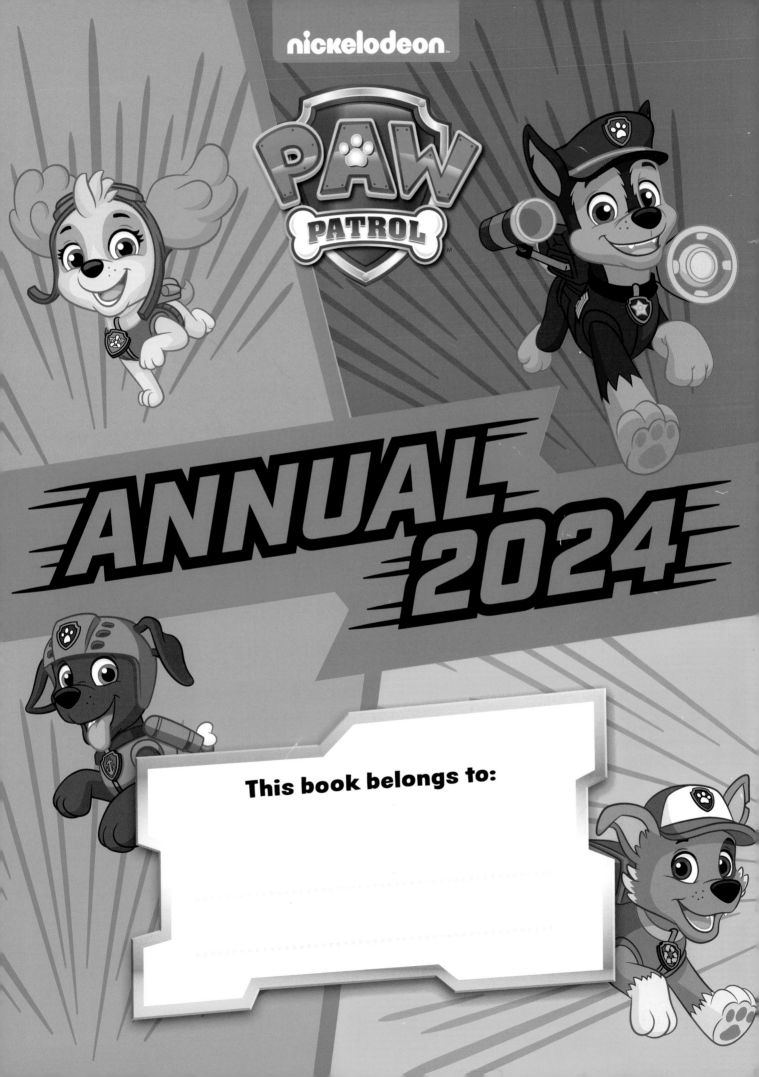

ANNUAL 2024

This book belongs to:

Contents

A Ruff-Ruff Welcome!

Trace the first letter of each pup's name.

Everest

Zuma

Rocky

Ryder

Marshall

Skye

Chase

Rubble

Are **you** ready to play in Adventure Bay? Turn the pages to discover puzzles, activities and stories, and meet all your favourite pups! Together with Ryder, they make the **PAWfect team!**

I Spy with Skye

Skye and Ryder are playing I Spy. You can join in too! Help them find **six things** beginning with the **letter 'S'** in the big picture.

Tick the boxes as you find each thing, then try writing the **letter 'S'**.

oap   un   weets

ponge

ock

trawberries

The answers are on page 69.

Count and Colour

Chase is busy counting everything he needs for his next rescue. Can you help? Count how many of each item he has, then colour in the correct number.

a

1 2 3

b

5 6 7

c

3 4 5

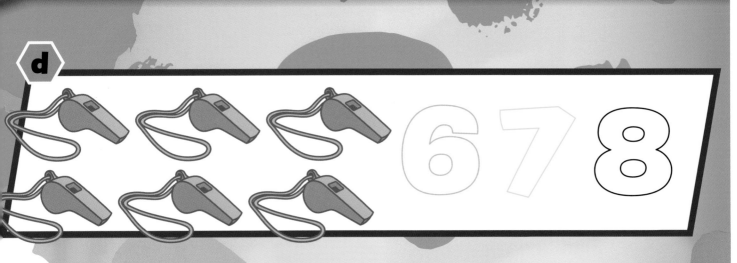

d

6 7 8

e

5
6
7

f

2 3 4

The answers are on page 69.

Rhyme with Rocky

Rocky is thinking of things that rhyme. Say the words out loud, then cross out the picture that sounds different from the others.

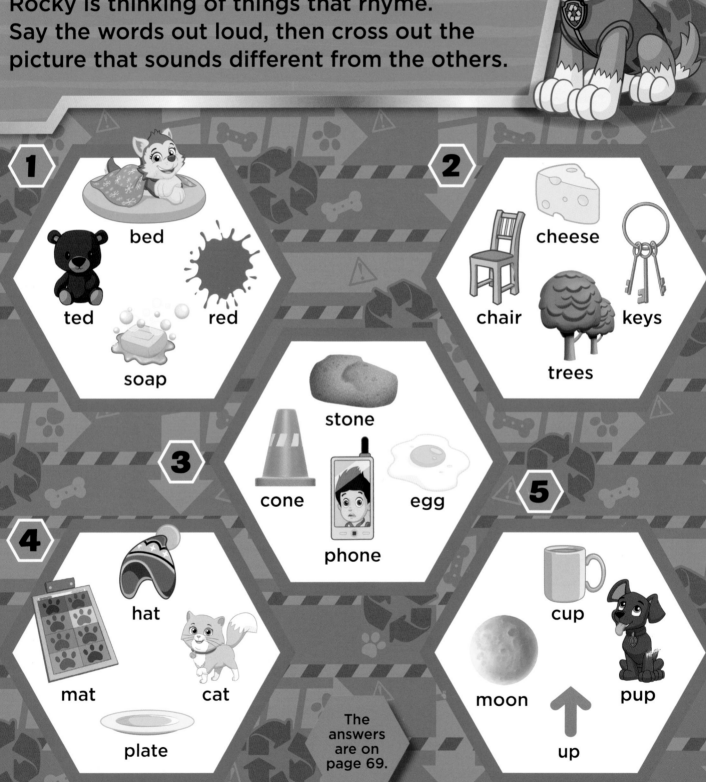

1.
bed
ted
red
soap

2.
cheese
chair
keys
trees

3.
stone
cone
egg
phone

4.
hat
mat
cat
plate

5.
cup
moon
pup
up

The answers are on page 69.

12

Tool Trouble

Rocky and Ryder keep their tools nice and tidy! Draw lines to match each tool to its shadow. Which tool doesn't have a shadow? Circle it below.

The answers are on page 69.

13

On a Roll!

Grab a dice and some pens or crayons to play this colours and numbers game!

Throw a
1
to colour Chase's uniform blue!

4
is the number you need to colour Rocky's uniform green!

To colour Marshall's red uniform, throw the number
6

Throw a

3

to colour
Skye's
uniform
pink!

Throw a

5

to colour
Zuma's
uniform
bright
orange!

To colour
Rubble's
uniform
yellow, you
must throw a

2

Pups Save the Bears

1 Mr Porter was trying out his new drone-powered delivery platform, when Alex spotted some big pawprints in the snow. "I wonder who made those?" he said.

2 They looked around to see what could have made the prints. "Over there!" shouted Alex, spotting a huge papa bear fast asleep.

3 Meanwhile, when Katie and Cali arrived at the Pet Parlour, they were greeted by a huge snore. "A mama bear is asleep in the bath!" cried Katie.

4 Across town, Cap'n Turbot was on board The Flounder when he heard a snore too. A tiny bear cub was asleep on the deck! "I'll call the PAW Patrol!" said Cap'n Turbot.

5 The PAW Patrol raced to Cap'n Turbot. Rubble used his crane to gently lift the cub on to a wagon that Rocky had built. "Good job, pups!" said Ryder.

6 Meanwhile, Everest had found the bears' cave. The entrance was blocked, so Everest used her Snowcat to clear it. "Ice or snow, I'm ready to go," she smiled.

7 The PAW Patrol rushed to Katie's Pet Parlour. Rocky quickly affixed wheels to the bathtub. "Bathtub to go!" he said, as the pups pushed the bear to the bed wagon.

17

8 Next, it was time to rescue the papa bear. "That big bear sleepwalked on to my delivery platform and took off!" Mr Porter told the PAW Patrol.

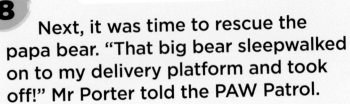

9 "Follow that bear!" Ryder shouted. The delivery platform landed on the Town Hall roof, with the papa bear curled up next to the bell tower, still fast asleep.

Get ready to slide!

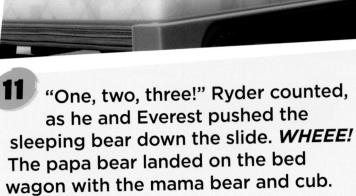

10 Everest and Rubble built a ramp out of snow to get to the top of the Town Hall. Then Mr Porter used his platform to lift Ryder and Everest on to the roof.

11 "One, two, three!" Ryder counted, as he and Everest pushed the sleeping bear down the slide. *WHEEE!* The papa bear landed on the bed wagon with the mama bear and cub.

❄

12 "Come on, pups," said Ryder. "Follow Everest to the cave." So the PAW Patrol took the three bears safely home to their cosy cave.

13 "If they get hungry, we've brought some yummy snacks!" said Alex. "Thank you for returning the bears to their home, PAW Patrol!" added Mr Porter.

14 "You're welcome," said Ryder. "If you ever find a sleeping bear, just whisper for help!"

Great job, pups!

A Helping Hound

Nothing stops this pup from delivering his load on time! Try drawing and colouring a copy of heavy lifter Al below.

Pup Fact

Basset hound Al knows his Big Truck down to its last lug nut!

Rollin' to the Rescue

Help Big Truck Pup Al through the road maze to Ryder.

Start

STOP
STOP
STOP
STOP
STOP
STOP

Finish

The answers are on page 69.

21

Heavy Haulers

The Big Truck Pups are ready to roll whenever there's a highway rescue! Can you work out where each piece goes in this jigsaw picture?

Now find where the pieces should go in this picture, so Al's Big Truck is ready for action!

2

a

b

c

23

23

1

2

3

The answers are on page 69.

Close-up Pups

Do these close-ups belong to Everest, Skye or Liberty?
Tick the right answer.

The answers are on page 69.

Here to Help!

The PAW Patrol pups are all special in different ways. Draw lines to find the best pup for each job!

A leaky tap needs fixing.

An avalanche needs clearing.

A heavy load needs hauling.

A forest fire needs putting out.

A new wall needs building.

The answers are on page 69.

Seeing Double!

Here comes Rubble, on the double! Trace over the picture of Rubble on the next page, then colour it in.

Pups Save the Farm

When Farmer Yumi and Farmer Al went on holiday, the PAW Patrol had to lend a paw!

Farmer Yumi and Farmer Al were going on holiday. **"Thank you for looking after the farm,"** Farmer Yumi told Mayor Goodway.

"You're welcome," said the Mayor. **"Chickaletta will be my super-duper helper!"**

"You just need to pick the carrots and feed all our hungry critters," said Farmer Yumi.

"No problem!" said Mayor Goodway, smiling. She waved goodbye to Farmer Yumi and Farmer Al.

Minutes later, Chickaletta hopped up to the barn door, and pecked on the button that released the animal food. She kept pecking until the barn was so full of food that the doors burst open and all the animals escaped!

"I'd better call the PAW Patrol!" said Mayor Goodway.

The PAW Patrol raced to the farm. Skye swooped through the air in her helicopter to rescue Garby the goat from the roof. Then Chase used his megaphone to round up the sheep.

Meanwhile, Farmer Yumi and Farmer Al had got lost in a fog. They stumbled upon Mayor Humdinger's secret lair, mistaking it for their hotel.

Mayor Humdinger was out buying cat food, so the farmers made themselves at home!

Soon after, he returned to find a strange truck outside his lair, so he blocked the entrance with a big boulder. Then he realised his precious kitties were trapped!

"Humph. I'd better call the PAW Patrol," the Mayor said.

Ryder and Rubble raced to Foggy Bottom. Rubble quickly moved the boulder with his bulldozer. The kitties ran out, happy to be free, while Farmer Yumi and Farmer Al wandered out behind them.

"Did you book this hotel too?" they asked Ryder, feeling puzzled.

The two farmers decided to head home.

"We realised we would rather stay at home with our favourite animals," they told Ryder.

Back at the farm, everything was tidy again and all the animals were happy.

"You really are a fantastic farmer, Mayor Goodway!" they said.
The Mayor blushed bright red and didn't say a word!

The end

Healthy Harvest

Clever Farmer Yumi grows all sorts of yummy vegetables on her farm! Look at the patterns. What comes next in each row? Say the word or try drawing the picture.

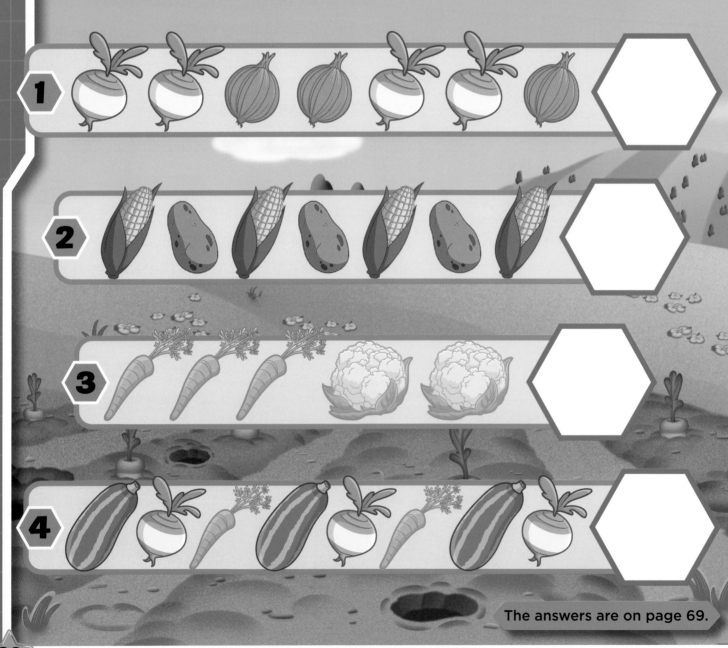

1

2

3

4

The answers are on page 69.

Starting at number 1, join the dots to find a crunchy surprise!

24
23
25 1
22 21 2
4
3
20
19
18 6 5
17 16 7 8
15
9
14
10
13
11
12

Ready for Action!

Rocky, Skye and Rubble are always busy pups, but what jobs are they doing today? Tick the right box for each pup.

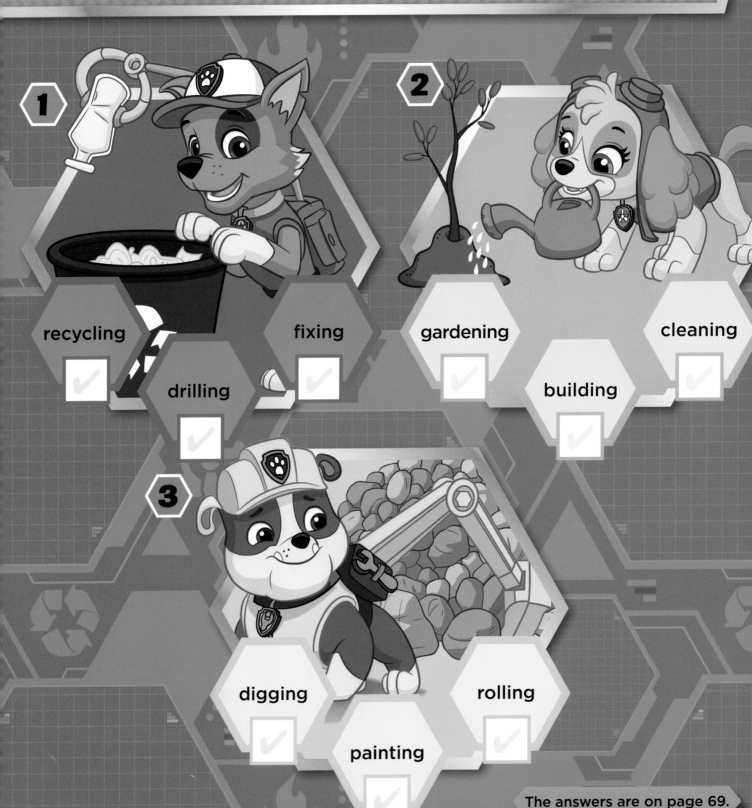

1

recycling ✓

drilling ✓

fixing ✓

2

gardening ✓

building ✓

cleaning ✓

3

digging ✓

painting ✓

rolling ✓

The answers are on page 69.

Taking Flight

Can you spot **six differences** between these pictures of Skye and her PAWsome puppy friends? Colour in a cloud for each difference that you find.

The answers are on page 69.

Chicken Run

You'll never meet a more curious bird than Chickaletta. Mayor Goodway's chicken loves to go exploring whenever the mayor's back is turned!

1 **The Lookout**

2 **Katie's Pet Parlour**

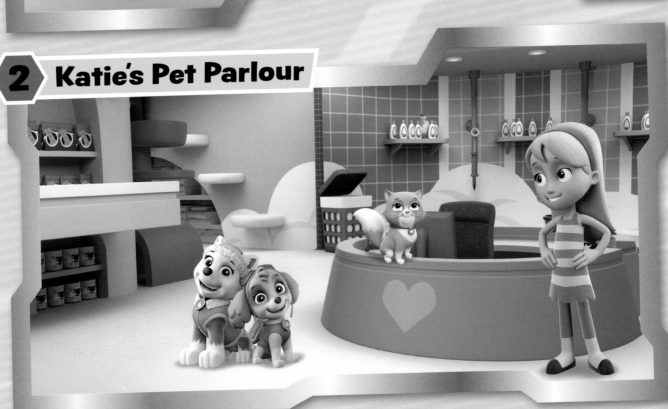

Can you find Chickaletta in each picture?
Say "cluck-cluck" when you spot her!

3 The Pup Park

4 Sailing the Seas

The answers are on page 69.

Meet CLAW

Claw was on his way to becoming Barkingburg's greatest knight, until he broke the kingdom's most important law – he captured a dragon to ride!

Breed:
Doberman
Armour colour:
Silver and purple
Did you know?
Claw made friends with Sparks the dragon by feeding him marshmallows!

"Sir Claw: the one and only!"

Meet SWEETIE

Sassy royal pup **Sweetie** is always up to tricks. Don't be fooled by her puppy-dog eyes or sweet smile – she'll stop at nothing on her quest to become **Queen of Barkingburg!**

Breed:
Highland Terrier
Armour colour:
Pink and black
Did you know?
Sweetie has a robot toy frog called Buzby.

"I'm one royal pup!"

Race to the Castle!

Heroes by day, heroes by knight! Race to the finish to save Barkingburg from Claw, Sweetie and Sparks the dragon.

You will Need:
- a dice
- a counter for each player

How to Play:

- Place your counters at the **START**.
- Take it in turns to throw the dice and move around the board.
- If you land on a gold space, follow the instructions.
- The winner is the player who reaches the **FINISH** first.
- The youngest player goes first.

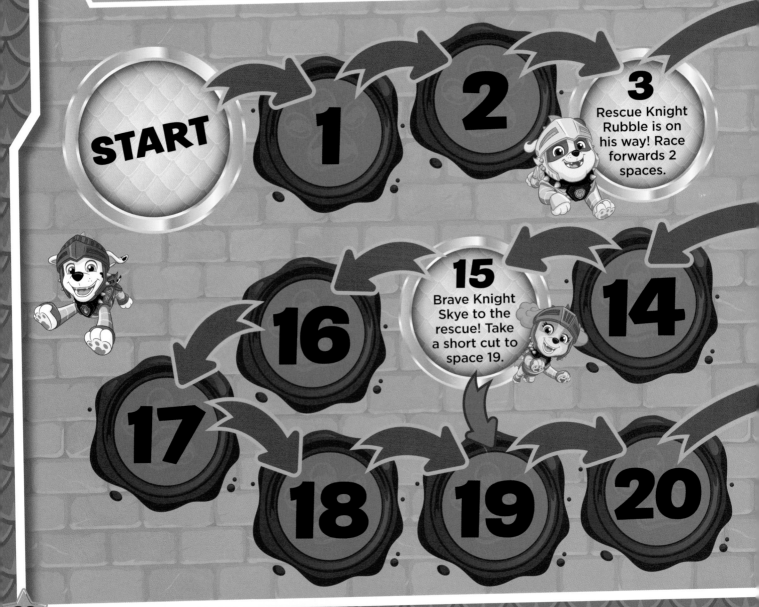

START

1

2

3
Rescue Knight Rubble is on his way! Race forwards 2 spaces.

16

15
Brave Knight Skye to the rescue! Take a short cut to space 19.

14

17

18

19

20

Ready, Set, Get Wet!

Zuma is on an underwater mission! Guide him through the maze, passing five turtles along the way.

Start

Finish

The answers are on page 69.

Pups Stop a Humdinger Horde!

1 At the beach, Mayor Humdinger's nephew Harold was hunting for a chunk of meteor rock. "If I find one, I'll get super powers and everybody will do what I say!" he said.

2 Suddenly, Harold spotted a glowing shell. Inside the shell was a piece of meteor. When Harold picked it up, his hands started to glow. "I'm super-powered!" he said, amazed.

My super cloning machine is complete!

BOOM!

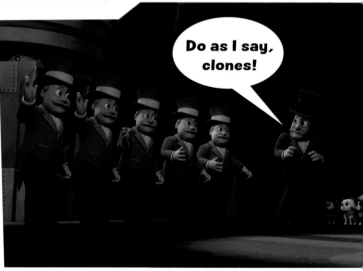

Do as I say, clones!

3 Harold used his powers to build a cloning machine that would make copies of himself. But while he wasn't looking, Mayor Humdinger sneaked into the machine!

4 Mayor Humdinger pressed a button inside the machine. Five exact copies of himself appeared. "What handsome fellows!" he said, sending the clones off to work.

42

5 The clones' first job was to bring Katie's Pet Parlour to Mayor Humdinger. But Katie and Cali were still inside! "Stop!" yelled Katie. "I'm calling the PAW Patrol."

6 "No mayors are too many, no pup is too small!" said Ryder. He quickly called the pups to the Lookout, where the meteor super-charged them into Mighty Pups!

7 Mighty Chase used his Super Speed to catch up with the clones, only to find that they had pushed the Pet Parlour off the edge of a cliff. Was Mighty Chase too late?

43

WHOOSH!

8 Luckily, the Pet Parlour landed on a ledge below. "That was close!" said Katie. Then Mighty Marshall used his powers to rescue Katie with a super-jump.

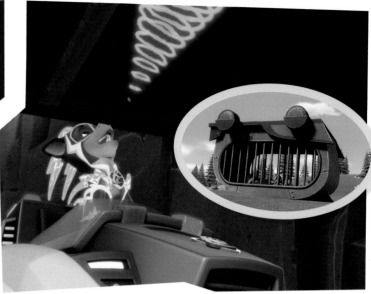

9 Next, Mighty Chase used his Sonic Bark to blast the Pet Parlour back to safety. Meanwhile, Mighty Rubble created a sonic ground blast to trap the mayor clones and Harold, chasing behind them.

Get us out of here!

10 In the blast, Harold dropped his piece of meteor. "Worst super day ever," he moaned. "I've lost all my super powers!"

11 Later, in Foggy Bottom, Alex ordered all the mayor clones back inside the cloning machine, where they quickly disappeared. "They were so beautiful!" sighed Mayor Humdinger.

12 Then the kitties began jumping on the machine until it broke into pieces. "Looks like your kitties don't want the clones back either!" laughed Ryder. "One Uncle Mayor is more than enough!" said Harold.

Nice work, kitties!

13 Ryder smiled at his team of helpful pups. "Too many mayors? Just yelp for help!" he said. The Mighty Pups have saved the day again!

Well done, Mighty Pups!

Snow Day

Use your finger or a crayon to trace the paths of Jake and the snowboarding pups as they whizz down Jake's Mountain.

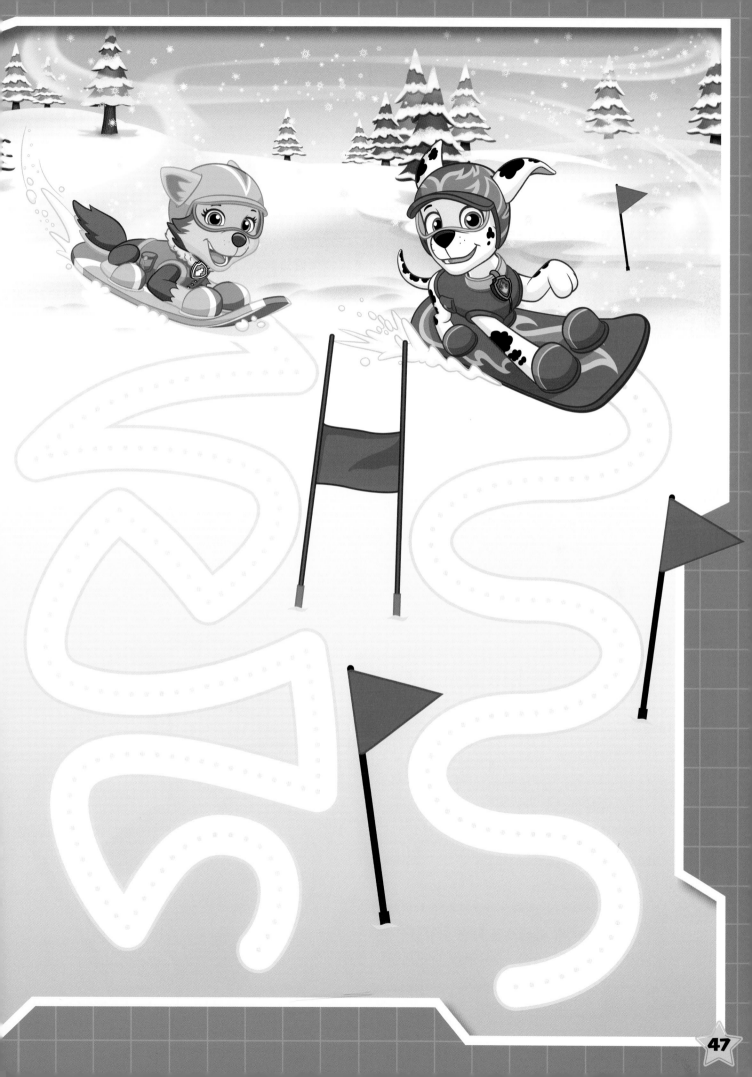

Bay Buddies

A friendly face is never far away in Adventure Bay! How much do you know about the people that live there? Answer as many questions as you can.

1

What is his name?
Mr Porter ☑   Mr PAWsome ☑

What is his job?
Shop and restaurant owner ☑   Vet ☑

Who is his grandson?
Alex ☑   Ryder ☑

2

What is his name?
Jake ☑   Al ☑

What is his job?
Mountain ranger ☑   Chef ☑

Where does he live?
Jake's Mountain ☑   Foggy Bottom ☑

3

What is her name?
Mayor Humdinger   Mayor Goodway

What is her job?
Mayor of   Mayor of
Adventure Bay   Foggy Bottom

What is her pet called?
Cali   Chickaletta

4

What is his name?
Farmer Al   Cap'n Turbot

What is his job?
Fisherman   Farmer

What is his boat called?
The Flounder   The PAW Patroller

Let's Roll!

The answers are on page 69.

Perfect Pup

Circle your favourite answer to each question to discover which pup you are most like!

Vehicle

1

Fire truck

Police truck

Snowmobile

Sport

2

Football

Snowboarding

Pup-Fu

Rescue mission

3

Clearing a big snowdrift

Putting out a forest fire

Making sure the roads are safe

Saying

4

My nose knows!

I was born to slide!

I'm fired up!

Friend

5

Ryder

Jake

Teddy

Colour

6

Blue

Red

Turquoise

Which colour did you choose the most times?

You are like **Chase**. Super smart, you can sniff out danger!

You are like **Marshall** – brave enough to take on any emergency.

You are like **Everest**. You love to play and help friends in need.

50

Marshall the Artist

Marshall is proud of his puppy picture!
Use your pens, paints or crayons to
show what you think he has drawn.

Three in a Row

Can you spot three of the same pup in a row?
They go across and down.

Which pups did you find three of? Tick the boxes.

The answers are on page 69.

53

Calling the PAW Patrol!

Who has yelped for help in Adventure Bay today? Trace over each name on Ryder's PupPad.

Katie

Mr Porter

Mayor Goodway

Lunchtime!

Rubble and Zuma are sharing their lunch. Circle the things they can eat and cross out the ones they can't.

The answers are on page 69.

PAWsome Puppets!

Here's how to make some fun finger puppets, ready for some new adventures! Ask a grown-up to help you with this activity.

You will need:
- 🐾 safety scissors
- 🐾 glue
- 🐾 card

Complete the puzzles on the reverse pages before making your puppets!

1. Ask an adult to carefully cut out these pages.
2. Stick the pages on to some thin card, then cut out your puppets.
3. Ask an adult to cut out the finger holes on each puppet.

Your PAW Patrol puppets are ready for action!

©2023 &TM Spin Master Ltd.

©2023 &TM Spin Master Ltd.

Adult supervision is required when scissors are in use.

Small but Mighty!

Ryder and his team of Mighty Pups are the greatest superheroes Adventure Bay has ever seen! Tick which Mighty Pup the super badge belongs to each time.

1 Give this Mighty Pup a Mighty Wave!

2 This powerful pup has Super Strength!

3 A Mighty Pup with Whirlwind Power!

4 Green means glow to this Mighty Pup!

5 This Mighty Pup is the leader of the pack!

6 A Mighty Pup with a Blizzard Blast!

7 This Mighty Pup likes to turn up the heat!

The answers are on page 69.

Pups Beat the Super Baddies

When villains Copycat, Harold and Lady Bird get together, you know there will be trouble!

Cap'n Turbot was getting his ship ready for a day of sailing.

Copycat spotted him and decided to cause trouble. **"I'm going to send that ship to somewhere only the PAW Patrol can save it,"** he said.

"We'll distract the pups," cackled Lady Bird and Harold.

Copycat used his mighty whirlwhind to send Cap'n Turbot's ship into a spin. It finally landed next to the crater of a tall volcano!

"This is a job for the Mighty Pups!" shouted Ryder.

While the pups were busy rescuing the ship, the baddies stole the mighty meteor, and with it, the Mighty Pups' super powers!

Without their powers, the Mighty Pups couldn't hold on to Cap'n Turbot's ship. Luckily, the ship slid down the volcano and splashed safely into the sea.

Meanwhile, the baddies were arguing over who the meteor belonged to.

Suddenly, they let go of it, and the big meteor started rolling down Jake's Mountain! On its way, a piece of meteor rock broke off.

Chase found the piece of meteor and the pups gathered round. Seconds later, their mighty powers were back!

The pups worked together and Rubble stopped the meteor in its tracks, just before it landed in the Bay.

Mission accomplished!

The pups made the baddies say sorry for almost causing a disaster. Soon, Adventure Bay was a mighty happy place again!

The end

Mighty Mission

Mayor Humdinger and Harold are trying to clone Ryder! But as everyone knows, there's only one real Mighty Ryder. Find the Ryder that matches the first picture.

The answers are on page 69.

Making a Catch

What is Cap'n Turbot's catch of the day? Follow the line to find out!

The answers are on page 69.

Toasty Treat

Ryder and Ace are toasting yummy marshmallows for everyone!

1

Can you spot six differences in picture 2?

Colour in a marshmallow for each difference that you find.

The answers are on page 69.

Giving Gifts

Ryder has wrapped gifts for his friends in Adventure Bay. Circle the biggest present and cross out the smallest present. Draw a line to join two presents that are exactly the same size.

The answers are on page 69.

Answers

Pages 8-9

Pages 10-11
a. 1 vehicle   b. 7 cones
c. 4 snacks   d. 6 whistles
e. 5 buckets   f. 3 pups

Page 12
1. soap   2. chair   3. egg
4. plate   5. moon

Page 13

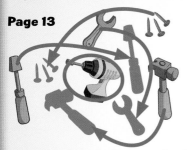

The drill doesn't have a shadow.

Page 21

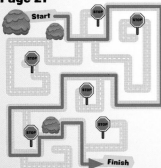

Pages 22-23
1. a – 3, b – 2, c – 1.
2. a – 3, b – 1, c – 2.

Page 24
The close-ups belong to Skye.

Page 25

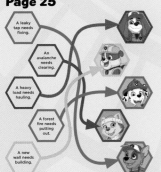

Page 30
1. onion   2. potato
3. cauliflower   4. carrot

Page 32
1. recycling
2. gardening
3. digging

Page 33

Pages 34-35

Pages 40-41

Pages 48-49
1. Mr Porter, Shop and restaurant owner, Alex

2. Jake, Mountain ranger, Jake's Mountain

3. Mayor Goodway, Mayor of Adventure Bay, Chickaletta

4. Cap'n Turbot, Fisherman, The Flounder

Pages 52-53

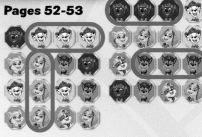

There are three in a row of Marshall, Skye, Zuma and Chase.

Page 55

Pages 58-59
1. Mighty Zuma
2. Mighty Rubble
3. Mighty Skye
4. Mighty Rocky
5. Mighty Chase
6. Mighty Everest
7. Mighty Marshall

Page 62
c is the real Mighty Ryder.

Page 65

Pages 66-67

Page 68
Biggest present = e
Smallest present = d
Same size presents = c and g